FLASH H

AND

MOST PECULIAR MOUSTACHE MYSTERY

by Karen Wallace

Illustrated by Judy Brown

Hodder Children's Books

a division of Hodder Headline plc

To Charlie Hurt, another rising star

KW

For Alan and Max

JB

Text copyright © Karen Wallace 1995
Illustrations copyright © Judy Brown 1995

First published in Great Britain in 1995
by Hodder Children's Books

The right of Karen Wallace to be identified as the Author of
the Work has been asserted by her in accordance with the
Copyright, Designs and Patents Act 1988.

10 9 8 7 6 5 4 3 2 1

A Catalogue record for this book is available from the British Library

ISBN 0 340 61960 0

Printed and bound in Great Britain by
Cox & Wyman Ltd, Reading, Berkshire

Hodder Children's Books
A division of Hodder Headline PLC
338 Euston Road
London NW1 3BH

CHAPTER ONE

Dong! Dong! Dong! DONG!
The beating of a huge brass
gong bounced across a garden,
halfway up an oak tree and
through the windows of a tree-
house that looked like a Swiss
chalet.

Inside the tree-house a tall
girl with a thatch of red hair
and eyes the colour of
turquoise marbles was reading
a book. The girl's name was
Flash Harriet. The book was
called *Subtle Solutions for
Super Sleuths*.

It was a thick, serious-looking book and the pages were well thumbed as if they had been read every day.

And they had been.

Because *Subtle Solutions for Super Sleuths* was written by Flash Harriet's uncle, a world-famous detective called Proudlock McCavity and on the front page were the words:

This book is dedicated to Flash Harriet, the most Effective Detective I know. Proudlock

Every time she read these words, Flash Harriet felt a blush of pride spread across her cheeks. She didn't make up Brilliant Noises on the piano like her father, Norman Brilliant, the composer. Nor did she walk on her hands along telephone wires like her mother, Sequin Cynthia, the acrobat. Instead, Flash Harriet had taken after her Uncle Proudlock and she had built up a reputation as one of the best detectives around.

Because, just like her uncle, Flash Harriet had the knack of sorting things out.

Dong! Dong! Dong! DONG! Flash Harriet shut her book and slid down the fireman's pole that she used for quick exits. When Norman was composing his Noises, it sounded like a tornado trapped in a piano factory, but when he beat the gong that meant one thing and one thing only.

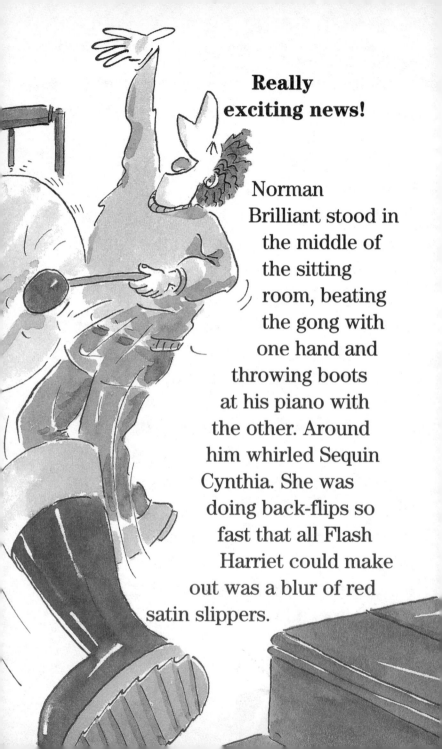

Really
exciting news!

Norman
Brilliant stood in
the middle of
the sitting
room, beating
the gong with
one hand and
throwing boots
at his piano with
the other. Around
him whirled Sequin
Cynthia. She was
doing back-flips so
fast that all Flash
Harriet could make
out was a blur of red
satin slippers.

The noise was deafening. Flash Harriet reached into her pocket and took out a heavy silver whistle. She put it to her lips and blew it as hard as she could.

"Darling!" cried Norman Brilliant, dropping his boot and kissing his daughter on both cheeks. "Such *exciting* news!"

"Absolutely *fizzing!*" squeaked Sequin Cynthia with a huge sparkling grin. Then she took a deep breath and held her arms by her sides as if to stop herself from back-flipping around the room again. "And such an *honour!*"

Flash Harriet looked around the room at the broken ornaments, the crooked pictures, the upside down chairs and the pile of boots that almost completely covered the piano. She had never seen her parents so excited before.

"What's going on?" she asked.

"You will remember my most recent Brilliant Noise," cried Norman, pressing his hands together and pacing up and down the room. "It was called *BOOING!*"

Flash Harriet nodded. For the first time, Norman had written a Noise with a part for Sequin Cynthia. As he and his orchestra played, Sequin Cynthia jumped up and down on a trampoline with special rusty springs - *booing, booing, booing!*

"Well," said Norman Brilliant,

going quite pink as he spoke. "We have been asked to perform *BOOING!* at the Ritzy Arnold Hall!"

Flash Harriet's heart went *bang* in her chest! "The Ritzy Arnold Hall!" she gasped. The Ritzy Arnold Hall was the fanciest place in London, where only the best people went. It was the sort of place you only ever *read* about!

"It's part of a carnival," explained Sequin Cynthia, standing on one hand.

"Festival, dearest," corrected Norman, kindly.

"Is anyone else performing?" asked Flash Harriet.

"One other," said Norman with a shrug as if such things didn't matter. "Heinrich von Beanztin played last night."

9

Flash Harriet frowned. "Isn't he the one who's always telling people he's better than you?" she asked.

Norman laughed. "That's him," he said. "But I don't mind."

"Logs and rubble," said Sequin Cynthia with a knowing look.

"I beg your pardon," said Norman Brilliant.

"Logs and rubble can give you trouble," said Sequin Cynthia, firmly. "But Heinrich von Beantzin is a nerd."

There was a short silence while everyone thought about this. "Quite right, dearest," said Norman, finally. "Let's hope the critics agree."

"What do you mean *critics*?" asked Flash Harriet, frowning. "Surely people don't come especially to criticize your Brilliant Noises?"

Norman laughed. "I certainly hope

not," he said. "Critics are people who come and listen to your work and then write what they think about it in the paper."

"Are they important?" asked Flash Harriet.

"Important?" cried Sequin Cynthia, walking across the room on her hands. "They're more than important." She took a deep breath and went bright red.

"They're *a matter of life or death!*"

"What your mother means," explained Norman Brilliant, "is that if the critics come to the Ritzy Arnold and don't like *BOOING!*, they will write nasty things about it in the papers and *BOOING!* might not be a success."

Flash Harriet looked from one parent to the other. She had no idea these so-called critics were so powerful. She made up her mind instantly to drop everything and make sure that nothing, absolutely nothing went wrong at the Ritzy Arnold Hall.

"*BOOING!* is your most Brilliant Noise, *ever*," said Flash Harriet firmly. "It will be a huge success."

"As long as I can find a violin player," said Norman, absent-mindedly cradling a boot.

"What?" cried Sequin Cynthia. She flipped back on to her feet, eyes blazing. "What's this about a violin player?"

"I need a violin player," explained Norman Brilliant. "My last one left the orchestra to become a bomb expert and there's a very important part for a violin player in *BOOING!*"

"Which is more than you can say

12

for the poor triangle player," whined a sour voice just behind Flash Harriet's right ear.

Norman Brilliant dropped his boot and looked up. "What's that?" he yelled.

"I said, I met a violinist the other day," said the same sour voice a bit louder.

Flash Harriet stared at the little man with the pointed face sitting in the corner. In all the excitement she hadn't noticed Silvery Ed. He played the triangle in Norman's orchestra.

Flash Harriet always felt sorry for Silvery Ed because Norman's Noises were usually so loud, no-one could ever hear the triangle. Now it appeared that Silvery Ed felt more than a little sorry for himself, too. For the first time, she noticed the mean look in his pale, pebbly eyes.

"And the violinist's name?" bellowed Norman.

"Johannes Meddlesome," said Silvery Ed. "He's world-famous."

"Fantastic!" cried Norman. "My dear friend! What would I do without you? Where did you meet him?"

"On a bus," said Silvery Ed with a small smile. "He's coming to the Ritzy Arnold Hall to meet you."

Flash Harriet stared at Silvery Ed and a funny feeling prickled at the back of her neck. Even when he smiled, the mean look in his eyes didn't change.

14

Flash Harriet didn't know much about violin players, but somehow she didn't think it was likely that you would meet a world-famous one on a bus.

At that moment there was the sound of five eggs smashing on the kitchen floor. It was Norman's especially adapted cuckoo-clock. As each hour struck, instead of making a boring cuckoo sound, the cuckoo popped out and kicked over an egg.

"Pulsating Pianos!" cried Norman, grabbing a fistful of papers, "we must go! The taxi is waiting!"

"Don't forget your waders!" said Sequin Cynthia. She held up a pair of stiff, thigh-length rubber boots.

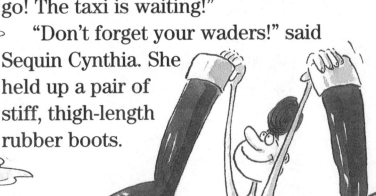

"The Ritzy Arnold is one of the oldest buildings in London and there might be..." "Don't say it!" cried Norman, his face turning as white as a candle. He took a running jump and landed expertly in each wader.

Norman Brilliant could take most things. But the fact was, that he could not take mice.

It didn't matter what *kind* of mice. They could be brown, grey or even a soft golden colour. They could have fluffy tails, skinny tails and sweet little black eyes. He hated them all.

He hated the way they skittered about on tiny pink feet; the way they squeaked and snuffled with sharp whiskery noses.

Norman Brilliant hated everything about mice. But, ever since an unfortunate accident when he had picked up the wrong parcel in a pet shop - thinking it was the sugar mouse he had just bought from the sweet shop next door - he hated *white mice.*

Flash Harriet raced across the

garden and up the ladder to her tree-house.

She opened the bottom drawer of her desk and took out a tiny red leather carrying case with wire mesh at one end. She unlocked the lid and gave a low whistle.

Across the other side of the room Gus, her pet tarantula, scrabbled down from his shelf over the door and jumped into the red leather case.

Gus had been Uncle Proudlock's idea. "Best guard dog you can find," he had said. And he had been right. But then Uncle Proudlock usually was.

As Flash Harriet turned the key in the tiny brass lock, she thought about the performance at the Ritzy Arnold Hall. It was vital that the critics liked *BOOING!* and that meant that

18

everything had to go smoothly. Which meant being there to look after her parents.

Flash Harriet smiled to herself. She'd been meaning to spend more time with them, anyway. The performance at the Ritzy Arnold Hall couldn't have come at a better time.

She looked through the wire mesh of the tiny case. Gus waggled a leg at her. "Glad you're coming too, Gus," she said softly. "I have a funny feeling I might need your help."

CHAPTER TWO

Inside the Ritzy Arnold Hall, it was all turquoise and gold, and glittered like cut glass. Flash Harriet couldn't believe her eyes. It was like being inside a magical paperweight. She looked up at the stage. Her father was standing in the middle of it.

"Norman!" screeched a voice that sounded like a train's brakes. "I *have* to speak to you, *now!*"

Flash Harriet dragged her eyes away from a pair of gilded cupids wrestling with a serpent which held up a chandelier. She knew the voice belonged to the beaky face of Vera Scrape who played the cello.

Vera Scrape was an old friend of Norman's but she was a stickler for *doing things properly*. And doing things properly was not something Norman Brilliant thought about much.

Vera Scrape folded her mouth together like a cardboard box. The truth was she didn't approve of *BOOING!* and she was going to make good and sure Norman understood this.

Norman Brilliant put down the length of rubber hose he sometimes used as a baton to conduct the orchestra. He was well aware that Vera Scrape didn't like *BOOING!* and he also knew why.

Vera Scrape was jealous of Sequin Cynthia. Which was absolutely ridiculous because Sequin Cynthia

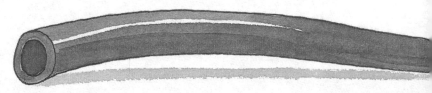

was not remotely jealous of Vera Scrape.

"Now Vera," said Norman Brilliant, smiling his most brilliant smile and bowing. "You know perfectly well I wrote *BOOING!* especially to give Sequin Cynthia a part."

Vera Scrape drew herself up to her full height. She was not quite as tall as her cello but roughly the same shape. "And you know perfectly well what I feel about trampolines," she said severely. "They are all very well in a gymnasium but they do NOT belong in an orchestra." She rattled the necklace of tigers' teeth she always wore and stuck her sharp chin in the air. "It lowers the tone for the *proper* musicians."

"And you, Vera," said Norman

23

Brilliant with a smile, "are the *properest* musician of them all."

Vera Scrape was not amused. "I am only here because I promised I would be," she said in an icy voice. "And I *never* break my promises."

Flash Harriet felt the colour rising to her cheeks but when he saw her, her father only laughed and took her by the arm. "Come and meet the other musicians," he said.

Stanley Dribble was a square-faced, serious-looking man with horn-rimmed glasses who, when he wasn't playing the trombone, spent all his time cleaning and polishing it. He shook Flash Harriet by the hand, nodded once, and immediately went back to work on his trombone.

Tubby Luscious played the tuba and looked rather like an overripe melon. He was large, squashy and sickly sweet. But he had eyes as soft as toffee and Flash Harriet liked him immediately.

At that moment a tall man leapt onto the stage. He was dressed entirely in black and had a curling grey moustache. He looked a bit like a pirate from an old Hollywood movie.

"Norman Brilliant, I presume!"

As Norman turned, the man thrust out his hand. "Johannes Meddlesome," he said. Then he bowed. "It's an honour to be here."

"It's an honour to meet you," cried Norman, clasping the man's hand. "I am so glad you were able to join us."

"A chance meeting on a train," said Johannes Meddlesome, smoothly. "A chance of a lifetime, perhaps."

Flash Harriet looked up sharply. A funny feeling was prickling the back of her neck again. A train? Silvery Ed had said ... But before she had time to think any further she found herself staring into a pair of eyes that were flecked yellow like a toad's. "Allow me to introduce my daughter, Flash Harriet," Norman was saying.

As she shook Johannes
Meddlesome's thin clammy hand,
Flash Harriet noticed that a strange
smell seemed to hang around him. It
was the strangest smell she had ever
come across and she had no idea
what it was.

"A pleasure to meet you, my dear,"
said Johannes Meddlesome in a rich
brown voice. "Your
reputation travels
before you."

"I do my
best," said
Flash
Harriet,
trying to
force a
polite smile
that wouldn't
come. She didn't

27

trust this peculiar man one bit.

"Indeed?" said Johannes Meddlesome, raising his eyebrows. "So do I, my dear, so do I."

"And so do I," cried Norman, grabbing Johannes Meddlesome by the arm. "Come and meet the others."

Flash Harriet watched Johannes Meddlesome glide across the stage, shaking hands and saying clever things. All the while, her father beamed and patted him on the shoulder. Norman seemed delighted with his new violinist. But then Norman Brilliant was like that. He was delighted with almost everything.

For a moment Flash Harriet wondered if it was her work as a detective that was making her feel suspicious. Perhaps Silvery Ed had just made a mistake about meeting

Johannes Meddlesome on a bus and not a train.

She looked down in the main hall. Silvery Ed was busy showing the music critics from the newspapers into their seats. For a moment, Flash Harriet wondered if he knew how important they were. After all, what they wrote about *BOOING!* in the newspapers would decide whether it was a huge hit or a total flop.

But Silvery Ed obviously knew about critics because he was doing his best to look after them. Each critic was handed a bottle of champagne, a box of chocolates and a frilly white pillow - just in case they got thirsty, hungry or uncomfortable during the performance.

Flash Harriet looked back on to the stage. Johannes Meddlesome was surrounded by all the musicians, talking and laughing. Everybody seemed to like him.

Everyone, that is, except Vera Scrape who stood on her own pulling at her tiger tooth necklace. Suddenly Flash Harriet found herself staring into Vera Scrape's hard granite eyes and her heart thumped in her chest.

Vera Scrape didn't trust Johannes Meddlesome either!

A bell rang in the hall. The rehearsal was about to begin. Flash Harriet raced up to the Royal Circle, and waited for the lights to go down.

CHAPTER THREE

Halfway through the rehearsal, Flash Harriet put down her binoculars and sighed with relief. Everything seemed to be going perfectly.

Below her, there was a steady sound of corks popping and chocolate papers rustling. The critics were obviously enjoying themselves, and from time to time they wrote in different-coloured crayons in their important-looking notebooks.

On stage Silvery Ed had a huge smile on his face and Johannes Meddlesome seemed to be enjoying his violin part. It was a difficult part. The violin had to be played the wrong way up and twice as fast as everyone else was playing but he was doing a terrific job.

Flash Harriet looked at Vera Scrape's bad-tempered beaky face and began to wonder whether all her suspicions were groundless and whether Vera Scrape was just a sour old bag after all.

Suddenly Tubby Luscious lurched forward. He seemed to be choking on something. Then, to Flash Harriet's amazement, thousands of coloured bubbles rose out of the end of his tuba and floated in twinkling clouds across the stage. Flash Harriet looked through her binoculars at Tubby

Luscious. The taste of soap in his
mouth must have been terrible
because his face was twisted and
pulled out of shape as he fought to
keep playing. Then she noticed his
eyes pop open as he looked sideways
at Stanley Dribble.

Toothpaste was coming out of the
end of Stanley Dribble's trombone
and the noise it made was truly
awful!

Flash Harriet moved the
binoculars over to her
father. She knew
that Norman's
Noises were so
extraordinary that
bubbles and
toothpaste could
possibly be part
of them.

33

She held her breath as she watched her father's face.

It was just as she thought.

The bubbles and toothpaste were as much of a surprise to Norman as they had been to Tubby Luscious and Stanley Dribble. But because the performance of *BOOING!* had kept on going, Norman, who liked surprises, was delighted. What's more, below her the critics seemed hugely impressed and began to clap their hands and scribble furiously in their important-looking notebooks.

As Flash Harriet turned back to the stage, she caught an extraordinary look between Vera Scrape and Johannes Meddlesome.

They were both purple with fury.

But what were they furious about? Was it about the toothpaste and the bubble bath?

Or was it something else? Like a plan that had gone wrong?

Suddenly Norman Brilliant went as white as a candle!

Flash Harriet grabbed the binoculars and trained them on his piano.

Her stomach turned over.

The worst thing possible was happening in front of her very eyes!

Two lines of white mice were marching out of either end of the piano. There was no running around in all directions like ordinary mice. These were trained white mice.

And someone had trained them on purpose! Someone who planned to wreck Norman Brilliant's performance.

As Flash Harriet stared, the two lines of mice crossed along the keyboard.

It was more than Norman Brilliant could take.

Disaster struck!

Norman Brilliant leapt from his stool, put his hands over his eyes and ran off the stage.

Flash Harriet watched with a cold, sick feeling as the whole performance ground to a halt.

But worst of all, she could see the critics muttering to each other and getting up from their seats.

"That was terrible," said one.

"Heinrich von Beanztin is much better, after all," said another.

The last critic had a bright red nose which glowed in the dark. He finished off his champagne and popped a final chocolate in his mouth. "Norman Brilliant has one more chance to prove himself," he said, picking up his frilly white pillow and stuffing it inside his shirt. "And I shall be here tomorrow evening, even if I'm the only person in the whole hall."

There was silence as the other critics seemed to be thinking about this.

Flash Harriet held her breath and hoped against hope. Then they all grinned and stuffed frilly white pillows inside their shirts.

"Come on," they said to each other. "Let's give Norman one last chance."

A minute later the Ritzy Arnold Hall was completely empty.

Flash Harriet ran down to the stage and stood on her own staring at the empty stool in front of Norman's piano.

Three words filled her mind and seemed to echo around the huge hall.

ONE...LAST...CHANCE.

Flash Harriet's turquoise eyes glowed like blowlamps. Tomorrow evening she would make good and sure Norman got his one last chance.

And this time there would be no bubbles, no toothpaste and no trained white mice.

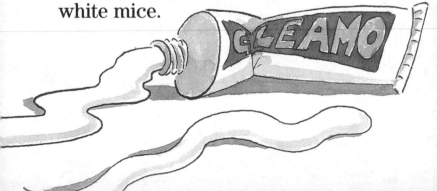

CHAPTER FOUR

That night in her hotel bedroom, Flash Harriet woke up to hear her parents moving about. She looked at her watch. It was well past midnight.

Ever since the disastrous end of his rehearsal, Norman Brilliant had shut himself in his room refusing to speak to anyone. Finally he had let Sequin Cynthia in on one condition, that she brought him a homemade toasted tuna fish salad sandwich and didn't say anything about what had happened.

Sequin Cynthia had made the sandwich and since then everything had been quiet.

Now Flash Harriet jumped out of bed and pressed her ear to the adjoining door. She heard the unmistakeable sound of Norman getting into his waders - a short run and a second later two thumps as he landed.

Flash Harriet dressed quickly. If her father was wearing his gumboots that could only mean one thing. Her parents were going out. And even though sneaking after them was not an easy thing to do, Flash Harriet knew she had to. They might just lead

her to a clue which would help track down whoever was trying to sabotage their big break.

Flash Harriet crept down the stairs and watched her parents slip out through the front door of the hotel. She could see Norman was carrying something large and heavy while Sequin Cynthia seemed to be holding a red plastic container.

They turned left along the street. Behind them Flash Harriet ran through the open door and ducked behind a dustbin. In the orange glow of a street lamp she could see quite clearly what her father was carrying.

It was a chainsaw!

Her heart leapt into her mouth as she saw them cross the road and open the stage door to the Ritzy Arnold Hall.

What on earth could they be doing with a chainsaw in the middle of the night? As soon as the door closed behind them, Flash Harriet raced down the street after them.

But just as she was opening the stage door, she saw another door that led directly to the main hall shutting behind them. There was a *clunk* as a heavy key was turned in the lock!

For the second time that night, Flash Harriet pressed her ear to a door. Only this time what she heard made her blood run cold.

It was the sound of a chainsaw cutting through wood!

Norman Brilliant was destroying his own piano!

Flash Harriet turned and raced back to the street. There was only one person who would know what to do now. She had to get through to her Uncle Proudlock McCavity!

Flash Harriet ran to the first telephone box she could find and dialled the number she always kept in her head. The telephone rang and rang and rang.

She was just about to put it down when her uncle's tape recorded voice simply said: What is it?

Flash Harriet had no choice. She left an urgent message and hoped her Uncle Proudlock would hear it as soon as possible.

WHAT IS IT?

As she walked back to the hotel she went through all the people who might be

43

trying to wreck her father's career.
She thought about Vera Scrape who
didn't like *BOOING!* because the
trampoline part wasn't *proper* and
she was jealous of Sequin Cynthia. If
BOOING! was a flop then Norman
would never write another Noise like
it and Sequin Cynthia would never get
another part.

Flash Harriet thought about the
extraordinary look between Vera
Scrape and Johannes Meddlesome.
Perhaps Vera Scrape was only
pretending not to like Johannes
Meddlesome. Perhaps they were
ganging up together against Norman.

But why would a violinist want to
wreck Norman's career? There was
always lots for a violin to do in
Norman's Noises.

Perhaps the real culprit was

44

Silvery Ed. Flash Harriet thought back to the moment when she had first heard him complain behind Norman's back about how he never got a big enough part to play his triangle.

Flash Harriet climbed back into her pyjamas. At least she knew she could be sure of Tubby Luscious and Stanley Dribble.

Tubby Luscious had complained all during supper about the taste of soap that was still in his mouth, and Stanley Dribble was in such a filthy temper about having to clean the toothpaste from his trombone that he had refused to eat anything at all.

As Flash Harriet switched off her light, Johannes Meddlesome's yellow-eyed face floated into her mind. And with it came the strange smell she had noticed when she had first shaken his hand. Once again she tried to work out what it was, or maybe it wasn't just one smell. Maybe it was a mixture of two things.

The haziest of ideas floated into Flash Harriet's mind. Maybe, just maybe....

She fell into a fitful sleep.

It seemed barely a minute later that there was a sharp knock on her door. Flash Harriet sat up with a jolt. Sunlight was streaming through her window.

There was another knock and someone pushed an envelope under the door. Flash Harriet jumped out of bed and ripped it open.

It was a telegram from her Uncle

Proudlock and it said:

TELEGRAM

NEVER TRUST A MAN WITH A FUNNY MOUSTACHE AND A FUNNY SMELL.

PROUDLOCK

Flash Harriet almost laughed with relief. The idea that had begun as a tiny suspicion had now grown in to a full-blown theory. Reading her Uncle Proudlock's telegram, she was positive she was on the right track. But even so, she had to make doubly sure nothing went wrong that night.

47

And that meant absolutely no
trained white mice.

Out of the corner of her eye, Flash
Harriet saw Gus taking his morning
walk around the ceiling. She went
over to the red leather carrying case,
unlocked the lid and gave a low
whistle. Gus scrambled down the
curtain and jumped inside.

Five minutes later Flash Harriet
walked through the main door of the
Ritzy Arnold Hall and on to the stage.
To her great relief, the piano was still
in one piece. She went over to it and
gently lifted Gus out of his carrying
case.

Gus was a guard tarantula. He
knew about intruders. And he'd
know how to handle trained white
mice.

"Thanks, Gus," said Flash Harriet

in a low voice, as she put him inside the piano. "I had a funny feeling I'd need your help."

Gus waggled a leg at her. Then Flash Harriet watched as he disappeared among the forest of piano wires.

It was a strange thing, she sometimes wondered if Gus actually understood what people said to him. But there was no time to think about that now. She turned and ran back down the aisle.

There was still lots of do and not a lot of time left to do it in. So far all she had were suspicions. What she needed now was proof.

CHAPTER FIVE

By the time Flash Harriet returned to
the Ritzy Arnold Hall every seat had
been taken and the lights had just
gone down.

BOOING! was about to begin!

Flash Harriet waited in the dark at
the back.

Minutes passed. But nothing
happened!

What on earth was going on?

Then around her people started
rustling their programmes and
muttering about wanting their money
back. An impatient buzzing spread
through the hall like a swarm of
angry bees. It grew louder and louder
and LOUDER...

Suddenly the curtain shot up!

Norman Brilliant was lowered from the ceiling wearing his waders, industrial gauntlets and a pair of brown leather horse blinkers!

As he sat down on his stool, Sequin Cynthia, in huge golden football boots, bounced out of nowhere onto the trampoline.

BOOING!

The performance had begun!

From the front rows, Flash Harriet heard the sound of champagne corks popping. The critics were back!

Everything went brilliantly. All the musicians were playing their best and the audience was enthralled.

Then suddenly, Flash Harriet felt a familar prickling feeling at the back of her neck. Something had gone wrong!

With her knees shaking she ran out of the Hall and round the corner to the stage door. Back stage, she pulled out her binoculars and trained them on Norman's piano.

To her horror, she saw two rows of pink tails hanging down from either side!

Flash Harriet's heart was racing like a speed boat engine. She

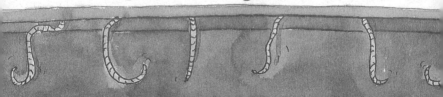

searched for Gus. Where was he? Something must have happened to him. Someone must have -

Then she saw him. He was inside the piano with one leg trapped between two wires! She watched helplessly as he tugged and tugged.

Along either side of the piano, the row of tails began to twitch. It was as if they were waiting for a signal.

At that moment, almost in slow motion, Flash Harriet found her eyes drawn across the stage to Johannes Meddlesome. A nasty smile spread across his face. She saw his arm raised to bring down the bow across the strings. And she knew that was the signal the mice were waiting to hear!

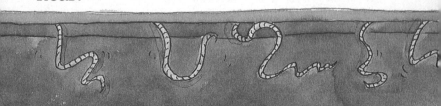

The second before the bow hit the strings, Gus pulled himself free and roared down the inside of the piano, his legs whirling like some monster satellite.

The terrifed mice poured over the side of the piano. Flash Harriet held her breath!

Just one glimpse of a tail and Norman's performance, in fact Norman's career, would be over.

But horse blinkers are big things and Norman was wearing the biggest ones he could find.

On he played, totally unaware that disaster was inches from his fingers!

Underneath the piano the trained mice re-grouped into a V-formation. Then they raced across the stage and ran straight up the trouser leg of

Johannes Meddlesome!

Johannes Meddlesome leapt into the air. His violin squealed like a pig with a tail trapped in a wringer. He started to hop all over the stage. And the more he hopped the faster he played.

Faster and faster and **faster!**

Meanwhile, Norman, scarlet with excitement, thrashed through the final bars of BOOING! As he leaned back to deliver the last blow, Sequin Cynthia bounced into the air, grabbed a rope and hurtled across the stage towards the piano.

The entire audience jumped to their feet!

At that moment, Flash Harriet noticed the piles of sawdust around each piano leg. They had been sawn right through! That's what Norman and Cynthia had been doing with the chainsaw!

Craassh! Norman banged the keyboard!

Thud! Sequin Cynthia kicked the piano!

BOOING! The piano fell to the floor!

The audience went wild! They clapped and cheered and stamped their feet!

But the show was not over!

Because Vera Scrape had realized that it was Johannes Meddlesome who had sabotaged Norman's Noise.

Vera Scrape might be a fussy old stick but Norman Brilliant was her friend, and she always looked after her friends. She stomped across the stage, picked up her cello and smashed it over Johannes Meddlesome's head!

Flash Harriet saw
Silvery Ed backing
rapidly into a dark
corner. "Stop that
man!" she shouted.
A moment later,
Tubby Luscious
and Stanley
Dribble
frogmarched
Silvery Ed in
front of Johannes
Meddlesome who
was lying on the
stage with his head
sticking out of Vera
Scrape's cello.

And again Flash Harriet noticed
the strange smell that hung around
him. Except this time she knew what
it was!

With one flick of her wrist, Flash Harriet ripped off Johannes Meddlesome's curling grey moustache.

The strange smell had indeed been a mixture of two things: glue for the moustache and cheese for the trained mice!

The entire audience gasped!

Johannes Meddlesome was none other than Norman's arch rival, Heinrich von Beanztin!

"Logs and rubble!" cried Sequin Cynthia, as she somersaulted through the air and landed on Norman's shoulders. "But Heinrich von Beanztin's a nerd!"

Norman Brilliant stared wildy around around him. "Will someone please tell me what's going on?" he muttered.

So Flash Harriet told him.

Heinrich von Beanztin had composed a symphony called *WIND AND TRIANGLES*. It was specially written with an extra large part for an extra large triangle. And that triangle was to be played by Silvery Ed.

Between them Heinrich von Beanztin and Silvery Ed had plotted to wreck Norman's career. Silvery Ed, because he was fed up with playing small parts in Norman's Noises. Heinrich von Beanztin, because he knew that Norman Brilliant was better than him and always would be.

At that moment the critic with the bright red nose stumbled onto the stage. His shirt was stuffed with at

least six frilly white pillows and he
had chocolate all around his mouth.
Flash Harriet recognized him
immediately, he was the critic who
had wanted to give Norman one last
chance.

Everyone stopped talking because
they all knew how important it was
for Norman and Cynthia that the
critics said nice things about
BOOING! in the newspapers.

Flash Harriet was so nervous, she
could barely speak. "Did
you like it?" she asked,
finally.

"Like it?" cried the
critic. "Like it?" He
paused to rearrange
his pillows. "It was
brilliant! Absolutely
brilliant!"

61

Flash Harriet sat behind her desk in the Swiss chalet-style treehouse. In front of her was a purple binder with FLASHBACKS written in gold along the spine. It was crammed full with all the cases she had solved.

She put down her pen and shuffled the pages she had just written into a neat pile. Saving her father's career had been a near thing but now that the huge success of BOOING! at the Ritzy Arnold Hall was in all the papers, Norman Brilliant's Brilliant Noises were universally recognized.

The extraordinary thing was that during the last performance Norman had hardly even noticed how near to disaster he had come. Instead, he had been inspired by the sight of Heinrich von Beanztin hopping about the stage and Vera Scrape stomping over to hit him on the head with her cello.

Across the garden floated the sound of splintering wood and twanging piano strings.

TWANG

CRACK

63

Norman Brilliant was composing a brand new Brilliant Noise.

This time it was called *Hop, Stomp and SMASH!*